Lost. Found.

MARSHA DIANE ARNOLD

PICTURES BY

MATTHEW CORDELL

A NEAL PORTER BOOK
ROARING BROOK PRESS
NEW YORK

Text copyright © 2015 by Marsha Diane Arnold
Illustrations copyright © 2015 by Matthew Cordell
A Neal Porter Book
Published by Roaring Brook Press
Roaring Brook Press is a division of Holtzbrinck Publishing Holdings Limited Partnership
175 Fifth Avenue, New York, New York 10010
The artwork for this book was created using pen and ink with watercolor.
mackids.com

Library of Congress Cataloging-in-Publication Data

Arnold, Marsha Diane, author.
  Lost. found. / Marsha Diane Arnold ; illustrated by Matthew Cordell.
    pages cm
  "A Neal Porter Book."
  Summary: When a bear loses his bright red scarf in the woods, it is
found—and lost again—by a series of animals that use it to keep warm or
to have fun, but they disagree over who really owns it and cause a
problem that only the scarf's true owner can fix.
  ISBN 978-1-62672-017-6 (hardback)
  [1. Scarves—Fiction. 2. Lost and found possessions—Fiction. 3. Forest
animals—Fiction.] I. Cordell, Matthew, 1975– illustrator. II. Title.
  PZ7.A7363Los 2015
  [E]—dc23
                                                        2015002341

Roaring Brook Press books may be purchased for business or promotional use. For information
on bulk purchases please contact Macmillan Corporate and Premium Sales Department
at (800) 221-7945 x5442 or by email at specialmarkets@macmillan.com.

First edition 2015
Book design by Jennifer Browne
Printed in China by RR Donnelley Asia Printing Solutions Ltd., Dongguan City, Guangdong Province
1 3 5 7 9 10 8 6 4 2

Especially for Neal Porter and Karen Grencik,
who brought me back into the circle
— M.D.A.

To Neal and Jennifer.
So glad that we found each other.
—M.C.

Lost.

Found.

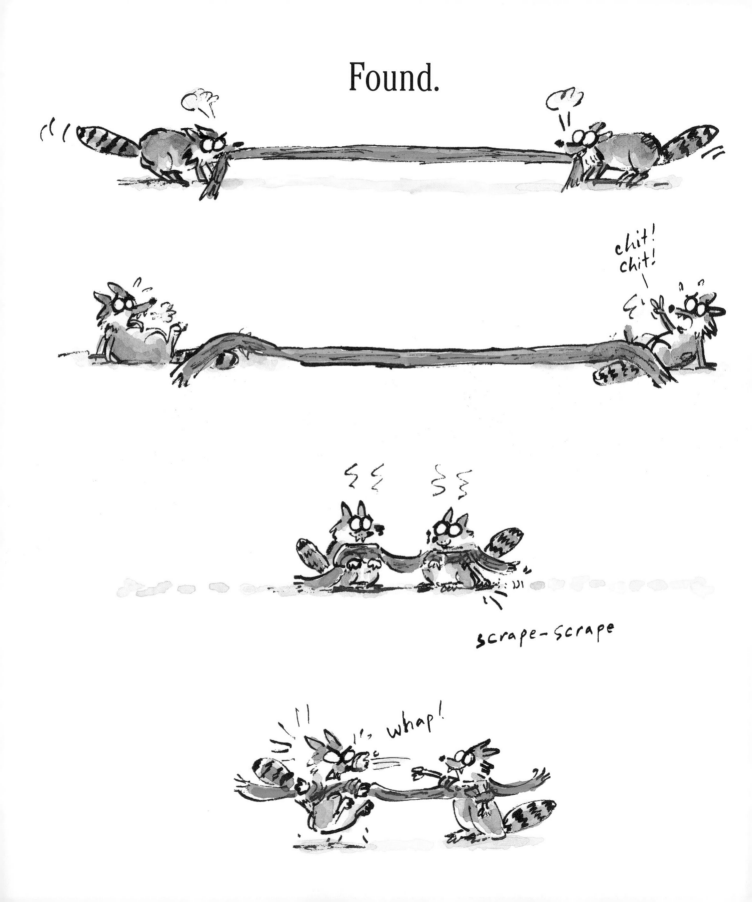

Lost.

Found.

Lost.

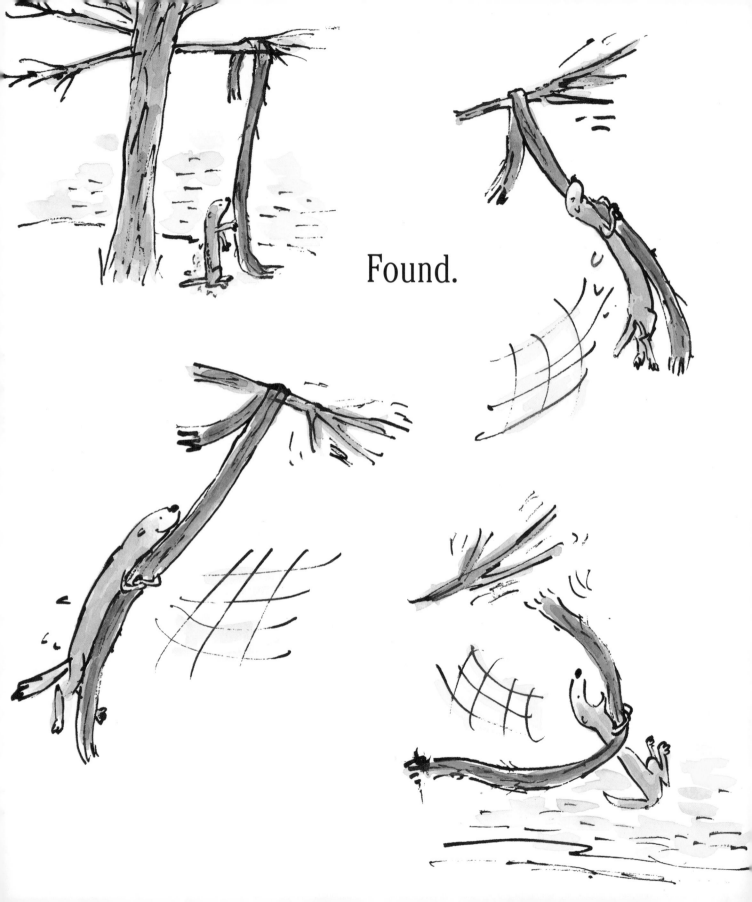

Found.

Lost.

Found.

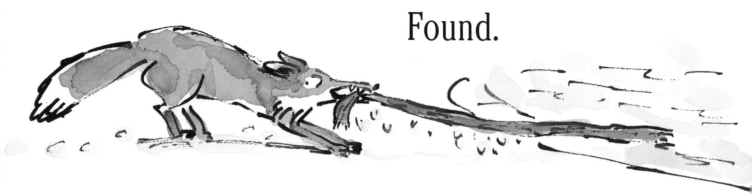

 squeeeeze

 drip   drip

Lost.

Found.

Lost.

Found.

Lost.

Found.

Lost.

Found.

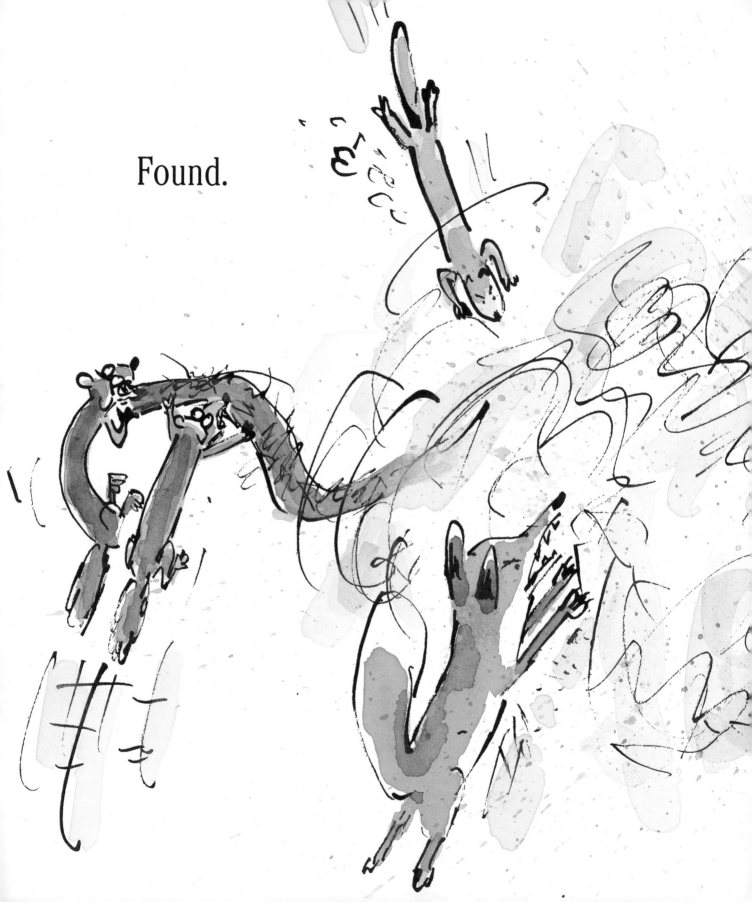

Lost.

Found.